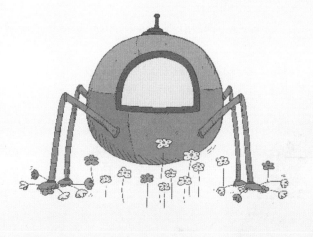

For M. Bryan - L.H.
For Mom - E.H.

Text © Longy Han, 2018
Illustrations © Elinor Hägg, 2018

Published by Pandasaur Pty. Ltd.
1120 Dandenong Road
Carnegie, Victoria, Australia 3163

ISBN: 978-0-9943413-2-7

A catalogue record for this book is available from the National Library of Australia

Typeset in Minion Pro.
Printed in China by Toppan Leefung Printing Ltd.
10 9 8 7 6 5 4 3 2 1

Learn more about *the Curious Travels of Gusto & Gecko* series at www.gustoandgecko.com

Gusto & Gecko
Travel to China

written by LONGY HAN   illustrated by ELINOR HÄGG

Pitter-patter, splash, splosh!

It was an ordinary Sunday afternoon.

Gusto and Gecko crept into the Rombom, their travel machine. Gecko burrowed deep into Gusto's pocket. "Prepare for take-off!" yelled Gusto.

Chuff...chuff...chuff. The machine sputtered.

It grumbled, chugged ... and *vrooooph*!

Off it went – zigzag, up and down, back and forth, round and ... *KABAMMM*!

Dizzy from impact, Gusto and Gecko wobbled out
of the Rombom.
"Where in the world are we?" asked Gusto.

The surface beneath them felt coarse and wiry.

The surface beneath them looked black and white.

The surface beneath them rumbled, and Gecko clung to Gusto in fright.

"Is it time?" asked Panda, rubbing his sleepy eyes as Gusto and Gecko tumbled down from his stomach.

"Time for what?" stammered Gusto, slowly inching away.

"The Zodiac Challenge. This year, animals from around China are challenging the twelve Zodiac animals for their spots on the Chinese calendar," explained Panda. "But I am not that interested," he added quickly.

"Why not?" asked Gecko.

Panda looked down at his paws and mumbled, "I am too big, too clumsy, too slow."

"But you would not know until you try," insisted Gusto.

"What if there is a bamboo eating contest?"

"True," said Panda as his stomach rumbled, "I am great at that!"

"Come on then. Let's take a look at the map and see where we need to go," said Gusto.

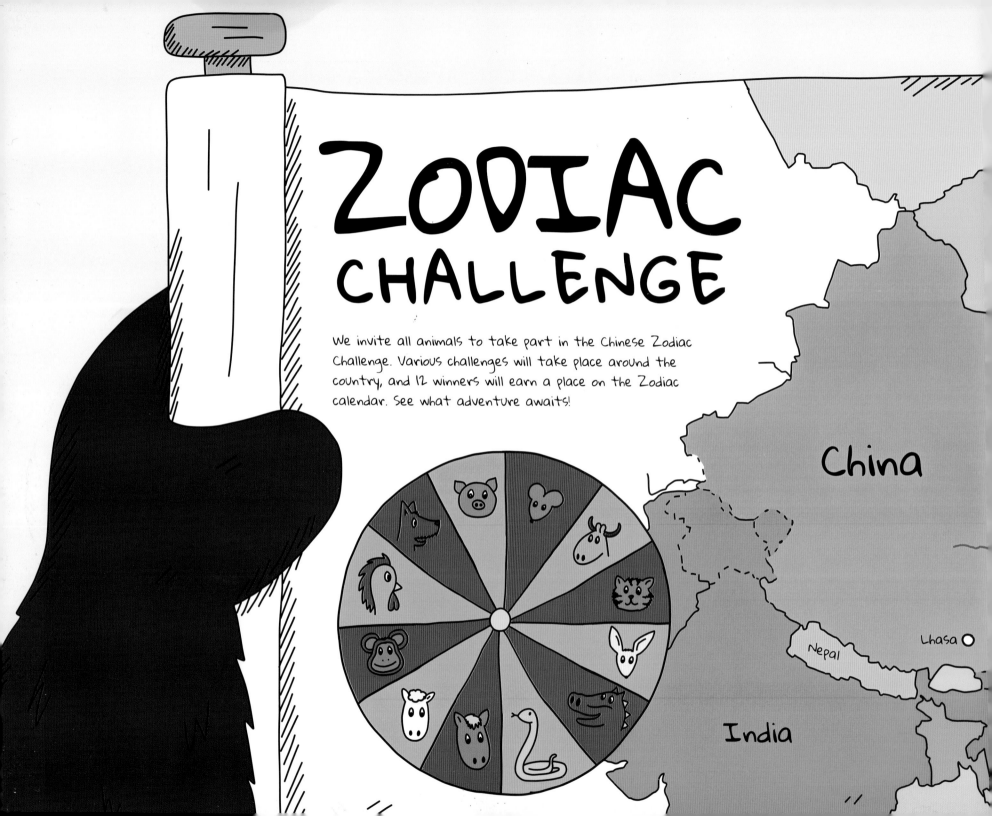

ZODIAC CHALLENGE

We invite all animals to take part in the Chinese Zodiac Challenge. Various challenges will take place around the country, and 12 winners will earn a place on the Zodiac calendar. See what adventure awaits!

China

India

Nepal

Lhasa

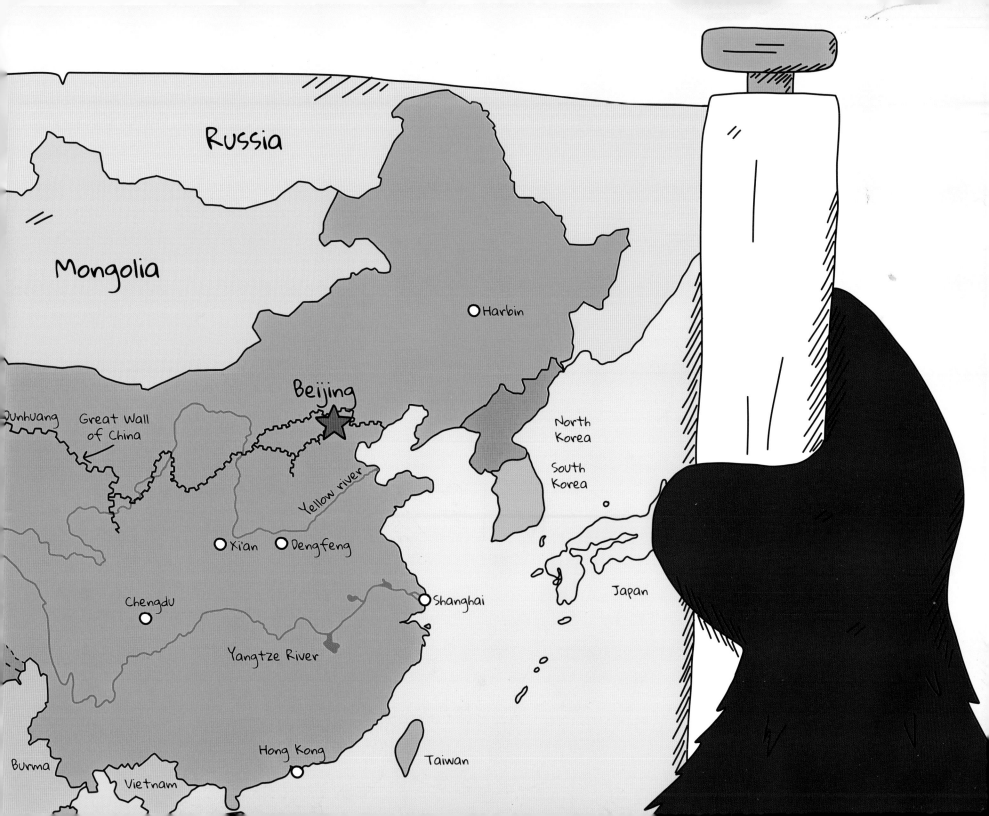

Location 1, Shanghai: Make Dumplings

Gusto, Gecko and Panda traveled to Shanghai to compete in the first task of making traditional dumplings.

"What do Chinese dumplings look like?" asked Gusto.

"Dumplings look like ingots, the money used in ancient China," explained Panda. "That's why eating dumplings is said to bring good fortune."

"Sounds like Italian tortellini, but luckier!" declared Gecko.

Along with the other animals, the trio got to work.
They prepared the fillings, and Panda demonstrated
his dumpling-making skills.

The monkey screeched that Panda's dumplings were ugly.

Panda flushed with embarrassment, and hung his head.

"I bet they taste like winners," Gecko said.

"Yes," said Gusto, reaching for the dumplings.

Om nom nom, nom nom nom, nom nom nom.

"Wait," cried Gecko as Gusto gobbled up dumplings. "You are supposed to be helping!"

Stuffed with dumplings, Gusto let out a loud *BURRRP*.

"That must be what winners sound like," whispered the rabbit.

Panda smiled. He appreciated Gusto and Gecko being there for him.

Location 2, Xi'an: Guard the Emperor's Tomb from Robbers

Next, all of the animals moved to Xi'an to guard Emperor Qin's tomb for a night. As the trio walked inside, their jaws dropped. Over 8,000 statues of terracotta warriors filled the trenches.

Gulp.

"Their different clothes and facial features make them look so real…" said Gecko in awe.

"More like super creepy," whispered Gusto. "I have a bad feeling about this."

The trio crept through the trenches, and stationed themselves in front of the unexcavated tomb. They shivered.

Then, the footsteps started.

They grew loud, and louder.

Close, and closer.

"You know Kung Fu, right?" Gusto asked Panda nervously. Panda shook his head.

Gecko, covered in goosebumps, whimpered, "They are coming for us."

Before the footsteps reached them, poor Gecko fainted from fright.

Gusto, shaking like a leaf, was paralyzed by fear.

So, Panda took charge.

He scooped up his friends.

He let out the mightiest *roar* he could muster and…

bolted out of the complex to safety!

Over the course of several days, all of the animals competed in different kinds of traditional Chinese activities. From writing calligraphy to hiking the Great Wall of China, from playing Majong to learning Tai Chi, from racing dragon boats to performing Chinese Opera, the trio tried everything.

Final Location, Harbin: Light Up the Ice Sculptures

On the last day, in teeth-chattering weather, all of the animals gathered in a dimly lit ice sculpture park in Harbin. Whoever gets to the main light switch at the top of the imposing lighthouse wins.

Some animals, afraid of heights, went home. Others, armed with ice picks and ropes, tried to scale the lighthouse but got stuck fast.

Soon, there were only a few animals left.

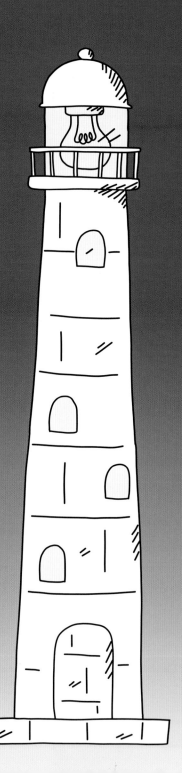

"How about pole vaulting?" suggested Gusto. "Or panda cannon ball?"

Final location

Harbin

"Or something more realistic," said Gecko. "Like working with other animals?"

"But it is our last shot at the competition," objected Gusto. "It is *us* against *them*."

Panda looked up, and looked around. "It doesn't always have to be that way," he said.

He approached the remaining animals to explain his plan.

One by one, the animals climbed onto his shoulders.

At first, there was a bit of wobbling.

Then, there was a bit of swaying.

Spectators held their breath as the animals struggled
to keep their balance.

Then all of a sudden, a magnificent light beamed out of the lighthouse.
A collective **Oooooooooooooo**
cut through the chilling air as ice sculptures shimmered and sparkled.
"We did it!" the animals cheered.

At the end of the contest, the top twelve animals were called to the stage. Panda wasn't called. Gusto and Gecko watched their big furry friend leave the auditorium, disappointed.

"We have a very special prize for a contestant who demonstrated exceptional courage, friendship, and teamwork," the judge announced over loudspeaker.

"Panda, you are the winner of the Animals' Choice Award!" declared the judge.

Cheers erupted, confetti filled the air, and the crowd carried Panda onto the stage.

Gusto and Gecko felt proud of their new friend. They waved farewell before returning to their Rombom.

It had been anything but an ordinary Sunday afternoon.

"Can we get some dumplings to take home?" asked Gusto.

Make your own Dancing Dragon Puppet!

What you need:
- Crayons / colored pencils
- Tape
- Scissors
- Glue
- Colored paper
- Two craft sticks

What you do:
1. Photocopy next page to use the dragon template.
2. Color and cut out your dragon.
3. Cut a strip of colored paper to match the width of the dragon's head and tail.
4. Make 'v' pleats in the paper.
5. Glue the head of the dragon to one end of the paper, and attach the tail to the other end of the paper.
6. Glue the clawed feet (also known as talons) to the body of your dragon.
7. Tape craft sticks to the back of your dragon puppet.
8. Move the craft sticks to make your dragon dance!

Tip: To make your dragon last longer, use construction paper.

'v' pleats

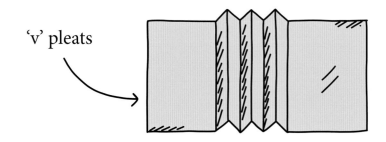

Visit our website: **www.gustoandgecko.com** for more arts and crafts activities!